A Gift For:

_____

From:

_____

Published by Hallmark Gift Books,
a division of Hallmark Cards, Inc.,
Kansas City, MO 64141
Visit us online at Hallmark.com.

Editor: Kara Goodier
Art Director: Amy Abernathy
Designer: Becky Hottel

ISBN: 978-1-63059-554-8
KCX1063

Made in China
0621

The Annual Snowville Frozen Fun Festival

Hallmark

A STORY FROM THE HALLMARK HOLIDAY SERIES
Written by Jake Gahr   Illustrated by Tom Patrick

'Twas the first of December–the big day was here!
The Middledrift family was filled with such cheer!
The Frozen Fun Festival was starting today,
and Flake, Fleck, and Fluff were all thinking "Hooray!"

Just then on the TV, a newsman appeared
and delivered worse news than they all could have feared.
"The Mayor and all of the Grand Snowville Choir
are stuck out of town with a blown-out back tire."

Flake, Fleck, and Fluff lost their feelings of zest—
the Mayor and Choir had to set up the Fest!
They'd hung all the lights since the whole thing was started.
"We may have to cancel," said Dad, quite downhearted.

"Snow no!" cried the kids. "We just can't let that be!"
They huddled a second, then shouted with glee.
"We know how to save it! Like you've said before—
If you need a friend, you just knock on their door!"

"We'll work as a family, we'll gather the town,
we'll get all the lights we find laying around,
and we'll make the festival happen this year!"
And with that, all the Middledrifts let out a cheer!

"We have to move quickly," Flake said, eyes aglow.
"Fluff, why don't YOU pull us fast through the snow?"
They hooked up their snowdog to two of their sleds,
and Fluff moved so fast their hats flew off their heads!

They went house to house, they went friend to friend,

they asked for their help, and then by the end,

their sled train had grown full of families with lights,

pulled by their snowdogs as day turned to night.

Now, off to town square the train raced through the snow,
and Fleck called out, "Let's sing a song as we go!"
And as their sweet singing soon rose in the air,
it seemed like the whole town of Snowville was there!

When the train reached the square, everybody helped out–
because that's just what Snowville is really about!
The parents and kids (and their snowy pets, too)
all joined in the festival hullabaloo!

They strung all their lights, both the big ones and small–
some twinkled, some blinked (and some didn't light at all).
And then at the end, overjoyed as can be,
the Middledrift family put lights on the tree.

When the townsfolk were done with the square decorations,
all smiling and singing in fun jubilation,
a big shiny bus pulled up into the square
and the Mayor and the Grand Snowville Choir were there!

"Snow my goodness,"
the Mayor said.
"Look what you've done!"

"The lights! Oh, how gorgeous! My gosh, snow much fun!

I'm sorry we missed all the great decorating!

But now that we're here, let's all start celebrating!"

With the lights shining brightly—as bright as their hearts—
the whole town of Snowville let the Festival start.
And they knew at that moment, more than ever before,
if you need a friend, you just knock on their door.

If this chilly adventure warmed your heart,
or if perhaps you just liked the art,
we would love to hear from you.

Please write a review at Hallmark.com,
where you can find more stories to share and love.